By Salt Water

Tales of the Sea

Shirl Knobloch

• • •

By Salt Water: Tales of the Sea

© Shirley Knobloch, 2017

Edited by: Jennifer Sabatelli

Cover, Photography, and Artwork by: Shirl Knobloch

ISBN 13: 978-0-692-86744-0

• • •

For Ingka...my friend by the sea

~~~~~~~~~~~~~

Sea Fever

I must go down to the seas again, to the lonely sea and the sky,
And all I ask is a tall ship and a star to steer her by,
And the wheel's kick and the wind's song and the white sail's
shaking,
And a grey mist on the sea's face, and a grey dawn breaking.

I must go down to the seas again, for the call of the running tide
Is a wild call and a clear call that may not be denied;
And all I ask is a windy day with the white clouds flying,
And the flung spray and the blown spume, and the sea-gulls
crying.

I must go down to the seas again, to the vagrant gypsy life,
To the gull's way and the whale's way, where the wind's like a
whetted knife;
And all I ask is a merry yarn from a laughing fellow-rover,
And quiet sleep and a sweet dream when the long trick's over.

—John Masefield

• • •

Table of Contents

. . .

Prologue

I wrote this collection of tales for those who yearn for the sea, for those who love the gentle beings who swim on the waves, the smell of salt in the air, and the healing winds that bring the most beautiful sunrises and the most colorful of sunsets...for those of us who must "go down to the sea again."

Where I Was Meant to Be

It was a blustery day on the water. Rough seas, fitting for the start of a rough few years of life. He had recently graduated with a marine biology degree from the School of Biological Sciences, Cambridge. He was smart, which was a good thing— he didn't have a rich family to steer him through rough seas on campus. But he was used to rough seas. His life hadn't been an easy one. No family to speak of, he was shuffled through the foster care system and luckily found escape in books and research and government scholarships.

He had seen the advert on the campus bulletin:

> *Researcher and ranger needed for a three-year study on the Farne Islands. Sparse amenities, harsh weather, and stormy climate. Job description: Ranger to Island tourists and researcher of the vast seal-breeding colony. Must be self-reliant and endure very limited human companionship.*

"Doesn't *that* sound great," he heard another reader mutter sarcastically to his friend at the bulletin board. But to Dylan, it did sound great. He didn't like people, never trusted them. Harsh sea winds couldn't hold a candle to the harsh words and beatings he had received as a child. He was always looking for places to escape—the library, the University, and now....The Farne.

He took a pen from his pocket and jotted down the application address. He had the requirements, surely, with his degree in marine biology. He was relatively healthy and didn't mind being alone; in fact, he preferred the company of island loneliness to that of a busy English campus or London research facility. He went to his room and started filling out the application immediately.

Age: <u>23</u>

Experience: <u>Degree in Marine Biology, Cambridge</u>

Reason for Application: _____

Dylan hesitated on this last one. Surely, escape wouldn't be a suitable answer. He had to come up with something really good. He did enjoy the sea and its life; otherwise, he would never have chosen marine biology as his chosen profession. The sea had been a source of escape since the time of pirates and smugglers off the English coast. He dreamed of pirates as a boy. He dreamed of tunnels in the rocks and disappearing on the waves.

Reason for Application: <u>I wish to fulfill a lifelong goal</u> <u>to understand the sea and all who dwell within her</u> <u>depths.</u>

He folded the application, placed it inside an envelope, and placed a stamp in the corner. He walked to the post and sent it off—**Farne Islands, Northumberland, Ranger Station.** Six weeks later, he received a call.

"Is Dylan Matthews there?" the man asked.

"Speaking," answered Dylan.

"This is Collin Frye, Northumberland Ranger Station. Are you still interested in the research position?"

Dylan's heart pounded. "Most certainly," he answered.

"Good," Collin replied. "There is a boat leaving for Farne Islands in three days, weather permitting. Can you make it?"

"Yes," Dylan answered, with nary a clue how to get to that boat.

Dylan went to the train station. "Is there a train to get to Farne Islands?" he asked the ticket master. "Yes, pricey though," he answered. "Will take you about five or six hours. Then, of course, you have to take a boat the rest of the way." Money was dear to Dylan; the price of the train ticket was just about all of his savings. Nevertheless, he purchased a ticket for the earliest seat on the following Thursday morning.

October 7, 1978

Dylan took a window seat. Long rides sometimes made him queasy. Funny thing for a marine biologist. He wondered about that boat ride soon to follow. An elderly gent sat next to him. Dylan opened his newspaper and feigned intense absorption in a story on page five.

"Where are you heading?" the old man asked.
Just great, Dylan thought to himself, *I am sitting next to a chatterer.* "Farne Islands," he muttered tersely.
"Farne Islands?" asked the old man. "Why, ain't nothing there but a bunch of seals and seabirds, and perhaps the ghost of a pirate or two. What would you be doing there?"
"I am a marine biologist," answered Dylan, a note of unpleasantness in his voice.
The old man grimaced, closed his eyes, and went to sleep.

Dylan shouldn't have rushed his breakfast; he felt his stomach a bit uneasy. But he kept his eggs down, thankfully. Five and one half hours later, the train rolled sluggishly into the station.

• • •

Quite a deserted station at that. Not a soul waiting or departing, just Dylan and the old gent. "Good luck with your seals," the old man waved. Dylan didn't answer.

"Which way to the landing to board ship for Farne Islands?" he asked the ticket master.

"The ship? You must be joking!!" the ticket master exclaimed. "Now there's Ted with an old dinghy at the docks, if that's what you mean. About a quarter mile up the road. Follow the coastline."

Dylan followed the coast, watching the sea birds fly among the rocks. "Are you Dylan?" asked a young man weathered by the wind and salt air.

"Yes, I need to get to Farne Islands."

"Come aboard!" shouted the man. "You must be the young Cambridge lad. Let's get you to that interview."

Now this wasn't going to be good. Dylan could already feel his stomach churning like the sea, and he hadn't yet set foot aboard the small craft. "Hurry up, the wind is with us," cried Ted. The little dinghy bobbed in the rough waves. *Great, I am going to die before I get there*, thought Dylan to himself, feeling his stomach about to exit his mouth with each bounce of the vessel. But the seaman was quite proficient; the two made landing in record time.

"Take some deep breaths. They won't be hiring you with that greenish tint to your skin," the dinghy's captain chuckled. "See that building on the hill? Easy to spot. Aren't many buildings on the Island. Just an old chapel and a tower and the island light. That tower is the Ranger Station. I reckon that is where your interview is. Good luck!"

Dylan could hardly believe his eyes. Hundreds of seals basked on the rocks. As many sea birds filled the skies above. Even his jaded heart had to gaze in wonder at such a sight. At the highest point on the rocks, a lighthouse stood solitary watch. "Something, isn't it?" called Ted.   "About 1,000 pups born here in the season. Kind of a sea paradise, don't you think?"

Dylan looked about.   Puffins, terns, all types of sea birds dotted the rocks. They seemed to have no fear of him as he walked beside them. Never had he been so close to a seal in the wild before. Here was a place where man could surely escape. He pulled his collar up around his neck. It was only early October, but it was cold. He could imagine how cold the winters were here.   He was glad to step inside the ranger office, a bright fire warming the air.

* * *

"Hello, I am John Fitzsimmons, Head Ranger here at Farne. Due to retire soon...these old bones can't take the winter here anymore. Sad to leave the place though. Been here 20 years, give or take a few." Dylan looked around the office. Not much to speak of—a tiny visitor centre with brochures about the wildlife on Farne, a few plush seal souvenirs, and woolen hats and gloves for chilled island tourists to happily purchase.

"So, Dylan, what brings you to the Farne?" John asked. "Me? I came to escape," the ranger continued. "Seems most come here to escape from one thing or another. I came to escape a lost love; she broke my heart and married my best friend. What's your story?"

Dylan wasn't the type to share life stories. "I have no loved one from which to escape," he answered. "I am not escaping. I am journeying to the sea and all its beings," he continued. "I studied hard, I am a good researcher, and I am not afraid of harsh living. The cold is not the only harsh thing in life."

John studied the young man's eyes; he saw something very familiar in them, something he had left behind when he first gazed upon the Farne so long ago. "It's yours if you want it. Best go home and pack up your warmest clothes. You will be needing them. And waterproof boots. The supply boat comes

· · ·

twice a month—make your provisions last. Bad weather can hold up the next scheduled shipment."

"I...I used all of my money on the train ticket here," uttered Dylan. "I don't have much to pack up home. I thought I would just stay here if you hired me." John smiled and said, "There's an extra cot in the ranger tower. I will be leaving in less than a week. I will ask the Wildlife Service Department to send you some suitable clothes and boots. Come, let me show you our research facility, although much of your research will be carried out in the field, or should I say among the rocks."

The ranger showed Dylan around the Island, explaining how to gather and preserve fresh water and store provisions safely and away from moisture (a hard task on this island). They shared a simple dinner by the fire. Dark came early to the island. A battery-powered generator was the only vestige of modern civilization. More weary than he had realized, Dylan went to bed soon after leaving the dinner table.

If dark came early, the mornings came even earlier. The rangers woke with the sun, setting about rounds on the rocks observing and counting the number of seals and taking note of any injuries or illness. Sea birds were also studied and recorded in the record book. Sometimes, blood samples of the seal pups were taken and evaluated in the makeshift ranger lab, John explained.

"The days are long and lonely," confessed John, "but there is always work to be done, Dylan. Are you sure you are up for this position? We hired someone three months ago. He lasted 12 days and then boarded the dinghy for the train."
"I am up for the job," Dylan answered.

In the following weeks, John showed Dylan all procedures and protocol. Dylan was a quick study; John felt confident that he could retire without worry. As Dylan watched his tutor depart for the mainland, a twinge of sorrow passed over him quickly. He wasn't used to such emotion. He brushed it off and quickly set off for his next island task.

Winter came soon. The winds and snow were unlike any Dylan had ever experienced. Provision boats were few and far between. Supplies were meager, and his bones were chilled to the core, but he fulfilled all his research assignments. Spring brought hundreds and hundreds of chicks to the rocks and sea birds scurrying through the skies and waves to feed their young. Visitors started coming to the Island. Dylan relished his privacy, but even he had to admit to himself that it was nice having a few humans with which to exchange 'hellos' and 'how are yous.'

He received a letter from John. He had settled in a small village in Cornwall, still close to his beloved sea, but not as isolated as the Farne. He had even started seeing a fellow church member, a widowed grandmother of three.

Summer came, and Dylan passed the nights reading. He had reconciled that a life of loneliness was his fated path.

October 7, 1979

A year had come to pass on Farne Islands. It was time for the seal pups to be born again, the busiest time of year for a marine biologist studying the fate of these beings. Each day was spent among the rocks, counting and recording all the pups. Soon, Dylan got so familiar with the pups that he could recognize certain individuals by their unique markings. Pups were measured, behaviors were analyzed, and feeding habits were studied.

One autumn full moon, a terrible storm crashed the rocks along the Island. Dylan was concerned about the seals and their pups. He knew it was dangerous to walk the rocks at night, but he set out by the light of the moon to observe the coastline damage. In the quiet of the moonlight, he watched several seals high upon the rocks acting in a most peculiar way. Hiding behind the rocks, he silently watched as, to his amazement, the seals shed their pelts and tossed them on the rocks. They were human! Somewhere, in the hidden regions of his memory, Dylan recalled a legend of the Selkies, but he never believed it was true. This must be a dream; it had to be. He watched them dance in the moonlight, laughing and singing and calling to the seals on the waves to join them.

How long he watched, he did not know, but he found himself on the rocks as the sun rose in the sky the following morning. *Have I been sleep walking*, he thought to himself. *This is not real. This is some kind of island madness.* He searched the coastline for any sign of humans but found none. He walked back to the ranger office and brewed himself a strong cup of coffee. John had a small library in his office with books about seals and sea birds and a few classic novels. There was also a book of folklore and fables. Dylan took it off the shelf and searched the index for Selkie. He read the legend and shook his head. "You idiot, there are no such things," he said aloud and tossed the book aside.

That night, the moon was still quite large in the night sky. Thousands of stars glittered in the sky, and Dylan could not rest upon his pillow. He donned boots and set out for the rocks. Sure enough, he saw the seals again. He watched them shed their pelts and hide them among the rocks. There were two men and one extremely beautiful maiden. She had long black hair and large, dark eyes that shimmered in the moonlight. He kept hidden and watched them sing and dance and run along the coast. Not knowing what to do, Dylan hid behind the rocks once again until dawn.

Back at the ranger office, he retrieved the book he had disregarded as superstitious nonsense and found the page about Selkies. *Selkies must possess their pelts to turn back into seals and return to the sea. Without their skin, they are trapped on land forever. During the time of the full moon, they come on land to dance and sing and take a human for their love. But to the sea they must return...*

Dylan kept thinking of the beautiful maiden. He could not get her out of his thoughts. He awoke to her face and went to sleep each night to the sound of her song. He planned and waited for the next full moon. He spent his nights digging a suitable hole beneath one of the floorboards.

The November moon was large and lustrous. Dylan walked down to the coastline and hid among the rocks. Sure enough, the three seals left the water and climbed the rocks. The two boys and the maiden shed their skins as Dylan watched. They danced beneath the moon and raced along the path toward the lighthouse. Dylan had to be fast. He dashed to the spot where the pelts were hidden and took the maiden's fur. His heart pounding and breath scarcely filling and exiting his lungs, he raced back to the ranger office and placed her fur inside the hole, nailing the floorboard over it again. Then, he ran back among the rocks and waited.

The trio returned. They went to retrieve their skins, but the maiden screamed. Her pelt was gone! They looked and looked. The two boys could not stay any longer; the sun was coming up. They donned their pelts and moved to the sea. The maiden watched in dismay. What could she do? She could not return to the sea without her skin. She was lost and alone and frightened. She had lost everything.

From the rocks, Dylan could see the worried seals watching. They were helpless, not able to help one of their own join them again. He heard the maiden make the most mournful cries among the rocks. She did not see him approach and tried to run away in fear.

"Please do not be afraid," he whispered. "Come, I will help you." He wrapped a blanket around the beautiful maiden and pointed to the ranger office. "Come stay with me," he said. "Be my love forever." The maiden cast a sorrowful glance to the waves and slowly followed Dylan. The seals watched mournfully from the water. They knew her fate—she could not return to the sea without her skin. This man must have taken it. Now, she was trapped to become his wife, his property, his prisoner of the shore.

"What is your name?" he asked. "Merian," she whispered. "Please, let me have my fur so I may go home." But Dylan did not answer. She was his now. He would care for her, perhaps even love her if his heart was able.

October 17, 1981

It was seal birthing season. Dylan was busy as usual recording the data. However, the seals never trusted him as much anymore; they knew what he had done. They seldom allowed him to get close to them anymore, and they sheltered their pups in his presence. Merian had become his wife, cooking, cleaning, and showing visitors around the ranger center. Everyone marveled at her knowledge of the sea, of the wildlife and the tides. She knew the restorative powers of the salt water; she used it at many times of healing on the Island. Her beauty was spoken of on the mainland by all who had seen her. When asked how the couple had met, Dylan's evasive remarks kept further questions at bay. Now, her belly laden with child, Merian was due to go into labor any day.

Dylan did not mistreat her. He gave her shelter, gave her food, gave her his idea of love. Still, Merian longed for the sea. She wept by the rocks each day, calling to the family she lost years before. The seals watched in worry, anticipating what would follow as Merian gave birth. But none could help her. All they could do was answer her mournful cries with their own.

October 19, 1981

The autumn full moon. Merian was in labor, and her screams could be heard by the seals among the rocks. At three thirty in the morning, a healthy baby girl was born. Dylan was elated. But Merian's screams continued, and eight minutes later, a silky baby boy with a shiny pelt of fur emerged. "What is this monster!" Dylan shouted. "Give him to me. I am taking him where he belongs, back to the sea."

"No!" Merian cried. "Please, he will not survive. Let me go with them, please!" Angered, Dylan ran to his office and tore up the floorboard. He took the seal pelt and went back to his bedroom. "Here, you want it? Here it is!" he shouted. "Go back with your monster, but leave the girl with me." Merian saw the pelt, felt the longing in her heart, and looked upon her baby girl in the crib beside her. With tears streaming down her cheeks, she tore a piece of her own pelt and wrapped it around her. Then, she grabbed her little boy and fled to the water. "Take care of her. Love her," she cried.

Dylan left the Island. He could not manage care of a baby daughter there. He went back to Cambridge and began a professorship in marine biology. His tiny baby, head full of lustrous black hair and glistening black eyes, was his pride and joy. He did love her, his Annabelle, and he taught her all he knew. She took to the sea; she loved to walk the sand with her father, collecting shells and asking hundreds of questions. She adored seals and had journals filled with their pictures. She painted pictures of their faces, and she continued on to write papers about them in college.

Dylan told his daughter that her mother had died in childbirth. And to Dylan, she had. He never spoke of her. He never told Annabelle that somewhere in the waves lived loved ones who would never see her grow. He never told of the patch of silken fur he had burned to ashes.

Annabelle chose Cambridge as her university, following in the footsteps of her father. She chose marine biology as her major and was thrilled to be the recipient of a study grant to do research on her favorite beings, the seals. Annabelle couldn't wait to tell her father the news. "Where is the study?" he asked with hesitancy in his voice. "Farne Islands," Annabelle answered excitedly. "I will live there for two years among the seals." "Annabelle, the Farne is no place for a young girl. It is too harsh. Please do not accept." Annabelle sighed. "Father, you have raised me to know the sea. I will be all right. Next Saturday, I leave for my research."

That following Saturday, Annabelle waved goodbye to her father at the train station. There was a sinking feeling of dread in Dylan's stomach as he watched the train disappear down the tracks. "Please come home," he whispered to himself.

Annabelle knew from the moment her feet touched the rocks that this was home. It was as if she knew this place, had felt the sand beneath her feet, had felt the slippery rocks and smelled the salt in the air. Fellow research students marveled at the trust the seals placed in Annabelle. They calmly sat for tests and measurements and weigh-ins. They trusted their newborn babies in her arms. It was as if she spoke to them with her shimmering black eyes.

One night, Annabelle could not sleep and decided to take a walk along the shoreline. Her long black hair shimmered beneath the moonlight, and thousands and thousands of stars twinkled above. Annabelle saw the silhouettes of several figures in the moonlight. Startled, she lost her footing on the wet rocks and slipped. Her head came down hard upon a sharp rock, and she was knocked unconscious for several moments. When she awoke, she saw a handsome young man leaning over her, tears streaming down his face. One of his tears landed on her lips, the salt water entering her mouth.

At that moment, Annabelle felt a strange tearing in her skin. It was as if she were a butterfly, emerging from her cocoon. Her hands felt soft fur across her chest. She tried to stand but couldn't feel her legs anymore. And in her heart was a longing to move toward the sea. "Do not be afraid little sister. It is time to come home. We have all been waiting so long for you." In the moonlight, Annabelle could see the shadows of scores of seals lining the beach, one of them missing a patch of silken fur. She could understand them; she was one of them. Her mother was waiting, the one with the missing fur. "Come, my daughter, come back to the sea. Come home." And Annabelle did.

The following morning, Annabelle did not show up at breakfast. Her room was checked—her bed had not been slept in. There was no way off the Island; no boat had docked last night. The coastline was searched, but not a trace of her could be found. Annabelle's father received the call from the police that afternoon. "Sir, we regret having to tell you about the disappearance of your daughter. Is there any reason she would take her own life?"

The policemen put down the phone and turned to his partner. "Now that was a strange question." "What?" asked the police detective. "Her father, he asked if there was a full moon last night. A full moon. Quite odd, don't you think?"

Tears of the Sea

Once upon a time, in a faraway kingdom by the sea, lived a lonely white dragon. She wept on the sand, longing for one of her own kind to love. But she was the last one of her kind; all others had been killed by man. So she wept, her large tears falling on the sand like raindrops. These weren't ordinary tears...no, nothing about a dragon is ordinary you see.

As she wept, she sighed, looking down at her glistening teardrops on the sand. Then, something magickal happened! We all know that dragons' breaths are fire. Her fiery breaths hardened the tears. They solidified into glass.

To this day, centuries upon centuries later, her tears are still there. When we reach down and pick up one, we must treasure it always. For they are what remains of her kind—beautiful tears of the sea. When you look upon a piece of ancient sea glass, you gaze upon a white dragon's heart.....the last of her kind.

Promise Me

C yril lived in a remote fishing village off the coast of England.   It was a poor place, a place from which people escaped......or people escaped to in times when too much of the world closed in on them.

He lived in a tiny cottage with his mother, Pearl. It seemed he never found his place, his purpose, his method of escape from the bleakness of his life and home. He was a dreamer, always thinking up a scheme to bring him fame and fortune. He was a wanderer, drifting from job to job, never holding one for longer than a month or so.

His mother was a quiet soul. She kept to herself. She must have been a beauty in her day, but now the sparkle had dimmed in her azure eyes. She loved Cyril as much as any mother could love a son, but love was not enough for him. He tolerated her, more unkind words spoken from his lips than caring ones. He complained of the food and the miserable cottage, but he offered no assistance to improve their lives.

Cyril's mother was becoming more frail with each day. They had no money for doctors—not that Cyril's mother would visit one even if they did. She relied on the remedies of the sea and shore. Regardless, her time was nearing, and she knew it.

"Promise me, my son," she pleaded, "when my time is near, you will take me to the sea."

"You are a delusional, old woman. Have you made anything for supper today?" he answered.

Pearl summoned all her strength and went to the stove to heat up soup. "This tastes like dirt!" he yelled. "What did you do, old woman, dredge the sand for seaweed?"

His mother softly whispered, "Please promise me, my son. That is all I will ever ask of you."

The following morning, Pearl could not stir from her bed. "Where is the coffee?" asked Cyril. Irate that he got no answer, he went to his mother's room. She was covered up to her neck in a blanket, her breathing shallow.

"It is almost time to fulfill your promise," she whispered.

"What promise?" he angrily asked. "Get the coffee," he yelled, pulling the cover from her.

Pearl could no longer walk. Her legs had fused together, forming an iridescent tail of shimmering scales. "Please, take me to the sea when the moon rises," she whispered. "Let me die in the sea. Here, my son, so you will understand."

Pearl handed him a letter, written many years ago, to a baby boy born out of love, love between a fisherman and his mermaid. *I loved him...I left my world for him. We had a beautiful son, and then my love went out to the sea one morning and never returned. I could not leave this world, for my son belonged here. One day, my soul must return to the sea, to my home and to the soul of my love. Without the sea as my grave, my body will burn to ashes. My soul will wander in the air, never able to rest in the water below.*

This was too much for Cyril. He left the cottage and walked along the coastline for hours. Then, his mind thought of a scheme. He could escape this hell now. Fame and fortune were waiting in that miserable sick bed back home......

Pearl died that night in that sick bed. Cyril called the media, the tabloids, and sold his mother to the highest bidder. They came. They photographed. They took her body to be examined, autopsied, her tissue placed under slides for *medical science.* No time was wasted; examinations of this strange creature commenced that afternoon. By nightfall, her body was placed in a research lab cubicle.

The following morning, researchers went to retrieve the waiting corpse, but the cubicle was empty. All that remained was a pile of ashes. The slide samples were empty, all photographs erased—no trace of Pearl remained. In the weeks that followed, a few lab workers quit. They worked the night shift, and in the quiet of darkened hours, they swore they heard mournful wailing through the building.

But Cyril had his fortune. He purchased a lovely mansion where the rich escaped. He traded love and promises for the company of friends who only cared how much he carried in his pockets, not what he carried or didn't carry in his heart. He met Sandra, a lovely, young woman, a woman who wouldn't have given him the time of day a few months ago. He married her and thought he was happy—until his pocket change jingled a bit softer and softer.

His health deteriorated, and his lovely wife paid him no heed. When the money paid to servants ceased, she would not even rise to make him a cup of coffee. She disappeared each morning and sometimes didn't return at night. Cyril was left to weaken and suffer in bed alone.

One morning, he felt something strange on his leg. "NO, not to me!!" he cried. "Not to me!" He heard the sound of Sandra's footsteps on the stairs. "Sandra, please come," he cried.

His wife entered the room, her lovely, blue eyes void of any compassion. "I told you of my mother. I told you how I made my fortune. Now it is happening to me. Promise me you will help me. Please, Sandra, take me to the sea tonight when the moon rises. I do not have much more time. You can have whatever money is left. Sell the mansion. You can have all that I own. Please, just take me to the sea."

Sandra didn't answer. She turned and walked out of the bedroom.

"Sandra, PLEASE, PLEASE, PROMISE ME!!!!"

Cyril worsened each hour. By sunset, his legs had fused, and he could no longer walk. When the moon rose, he heard Sandra's footsteps on the stairs. She wasn't alone. She entered his bedroom, a tall man beside her.

"We have come for you," she said. "I am Pearl's sister. This is her father. We told her not to leave our world, not to give up her home and family for the love of one who walks on land. But she didn't listen. Beings of the sea are connected. We felt what she felt; we saw what you did to her. We came to your world to fulfill your promise. We will take you to the sea."

"Oh, thank you, thank you. I am sorry. I am so very sorry!!" he cried.

Sandra and her father helped his dying body to the edge of the sea. There, a tiny boat was waiting. They lifted him upon it and tied his arms and tail down.

"PLEASE, I MUST GO TO THE SEA!!!" Cyril screamed.

"No, you shall never go to the sea. You shall die a cruel and suffering death upon her......may your soul wander for eternity."

With that, they pushed the tiny vessel out among the waves. Sandra and her father took the phial of poison. Together, they shared the bitter liquid. Then, they dove into the waiting currents. Those currents carried the souls of two mermaids home. Those currents carried an empty boat several miles down the coastline. Only a heap of ashes remained in her hull. On windy nights, villagers swear they hear the mournful wails of lost souls...a mother and her son doomed to be lost in eternity.

Her Birthday Wish

C eleste lived by the sea. She once lived in London, successful at her job in the stressful world of finance. But the passing years grew shorter and shorter, and in her late fifties, Celeste answered her heart's call to leave the city behind and settle in a little cottage at the edge of the world.

That was twenty years ago, and Celeste regretted not one single day. Not one single sunrise, with the morning birds and seals at play on the shoreline. Not one single sunset, with the sound of the sea tides—instead of the taxis and sirens of the city—to sing her to sleep each night. Celeste had many friends, but most didn't understand the move. Some visited every once in a while, but now, Celeste called the seals her friends. She seemed to understand them, and they her. She was at peace here; she didn't have to impress anyone or pretend to be anything she was not. She could truly be herself. And the seals accepted her for just that, the beautiful soul that she was.

She talked to them each morning, told them her deepest secrets. They brought her little gifts—the prettiest of shells, the most sparkling of sea glass, the deepest colors of coral. She often told them how she wished she could be one of them. *"I am old now,"* she would whisper to them, their black eyes looking deep into her soul. *"How I wonder what* awaits, if anything awaits, when my time ends here on Earth. Do you know what awaits, my friends?" she asked.

"It is my birthday next month. I will be 80 years old," she continued. "The saddest part of growing old is leaving all of you behind. If heaven is whatever our heart so wishes, I wish to be with you."

The seals watched their friend lift her feet out of the shallow water. Sadly, Celeste turned and walked slowly back to her cottage. The salt water felt good on her bones, but they still ached. Celeste knew her questions would be answered all too soon.

Seals are most intelligent beings. They gathered together and decided to make this birthday a very, very special one for Celeste. They had one month to accomplish it. They would need the help of everyone in the seal colony, and there was little time to spare. Word went out among the seal groups. Each was asked to donate a tiny bit of fur from their pelts, shaved off with a sharp edge of coral. The starfish were called in on the project. With their pointy appendages, they were expert spinners. The seals gathered twine from fishermen nets and carried it to the starfish with tiny patches of seal fur.

Spin this fur and twine it into a lovely patchwork quilt, and you and your children will never go hungry one day in the sea again, they told the starfish. Thinking such a good deal was foolish to refuse, the starfish started spinning, and spinning, and spinning. The seals brought them delicious morsels from the sea and more and more bits of fur and twine each day.

Soon, the quilt was almost ready. *It must be so beautiful,* the seals exclaimed. *We must ask the mermaids to help.* So the seals went off in search of the elusive beings and told them of their gift. *It must sparkle like the sea,* they told their friends.

Everyone in the sea knew that mermaids seldom cried, but when they did, their tears solidified into pearls. The mermaids were so touched by the seals' love of their human friend that tears flowed down their faces. Mermaid tears were filled with all the secrets and magic of the sea, for the mermaids had witnessed all, since the first waves rolled on to the sand. The seals captured the tears in large shells and carried them to the starfish. *Weave these into her quilt,* they requested.

The starfish spun and spun and spun and weaved and weaved and weaved. The quilt was ready. It was the most exquisite pelt of fur and pearls the seals had ever seen. The mermaids came to marvel at its sheen. *Celeste will love this!* they all shouted, beaming with pride.

Thank you, starfish, for your handiwork, and thank you, mermaids, for your tears.

• • •

The morning of Celeste's birthday came. London friends had asked her into the city for dinner and theatre, but Celeste was feeling tired and declined. Besides, there was only one place her heart longed to be on this day. Celeste slept late. The seals had been waiting and worrying for several hours. Finally, near dusk, Celeste slowly walked to the rocks and sat down.

One by one, the seals crept up to her side. Several carried a large piece of cloth in their seal fins. As they got closer, Celeste saw it was a beautiful pelt. "It is the most beautiful thing I have ever seen!" she gasped. The seals draped the pelt around her legs. Celeste took hold of it and gathered it up around her shoulders. "I cannot believe you have given me this treasure. You knew it was today, my birthday! This is so beautiful. I have no words!" Celeste stroked the silky fur. She caressed each pearl and lay down on the rocks with her quilt wrapped tightly around her. As the moon rose in the sky, Celeste lay very still, sleeping with more happiness in her heart than she had ever felt before.

When the sunrise came, the sea birds called. The seals were not among the rocks. And neither was Celeste. No one ever found her. The village notified the authorities who notified her London friends. "Strangest thing ever," the police said. "She was eighty, after all. Maybe she lost her sense of direction and wandered out to sea. It is as if she stepped out of her cottage and went to another world."

Celeste's file said *missing person*. But Celeste wasn't missing...the heaven of her heart had found her at last. And soon, along the coastline, a lovely seal with the silkiest of pelts could be seen sunning herself on the rocks beside her friends.

Story in the Sand

Mona walked the sand each morning as the tide receded. She searched for sea glass. To her, the smooth luminescence of sea glass was more beautiful than gemstones. She fashioned it into jewelry, into mosaics, into creative home furnishings, and sold them to tourist shops in her seaside town.

Each piece of glass held a story. It took centuries for authentic sea glass to be smoothed by the waves and sand. Yes, modern technology could create sea glass easily now, but the priceless pieces not so easily found these days were treasures to the young artist. Might this one have been a Roman vessel, holding wine in the courtyard of a wealthy family? Could this one have adorned the ears of a young maiden on her wedding day? Each piece of glass hid a story of centuries past.

Mona believed in energy. Each object on this planet held energy. Each piece of sea glass held energy. Within its smooth edges, both joyful and dark moments of history could be trapped. Under the full moon, she lined her windowsill with freshly found pieces to cleanse them of their history. She didn't want any of her pieces to bring bad energy into the home of a customer who purchased it in the village shop.

One day, Mona saw a glistening piece of green sea glass in the sand. It was such a lovely shade of green. *This one will be mine,* she thought to herself. She couldn't wait to walk home and fashion it into something of her very own. She hurried to her workshop desk, took out her jewelry supplies, and twisted wire around the piece of glass, fashioning it into a beautiful pendant. Pleased with her handiwork, she threaded a silken cord through the pendant bail and tied it around her neck. *So lovely*, she thought as she caressed the silken face of the glass.

Suddenly, visions danced through her head. Visions of fire, of explosions, of terror. Mona was frightened. She shrugged it off when her dog started barking at the mailman. *Mona, your imagination is getting the best of you,* she chuckled to herself.

She sat back down to work; she had two mosaic orders to be filled by the end of the week. She worked until the daylight hours faded and piecing the glass together became too difficult to see. She laid the beautiful pendant on her bedside table and drifted off to sleep.

Her dreams brought a beautiful place, a place of colorful mosaics on the floors and walls. She had seen these before, she knew it. Then came the terror. The running, the screaming, the burning of flesh. In the distance, she saw a volcano erupting, spewing lava and ash into the darkening sky. Suddenly, the alarm rang. Heart thumping, her pajamas filled with sweat, Mona turned to the bedside table to shut the alarm. Her hand touched the pendant.

• • •

"Where did you come from?" she asked. "It seems you are trying to tell me." Mona showered, dressed, and tied the sea glass around her neck. She sat at her workshop and finished the first of the two mosaic orders.

That night, the visions returned. She saw a lovely young woman, a woman carrying a beautiful glass vase of flowers in her hands. She was placing it on a table laden with breads and cheese and calling to her children to come to eat. A little dog sat up, eagerly awaiting a taste. Suddenly, a blast of tremendous burning air filled the room. Mona saw the vase lift into the air from the woman's hands. She saw the room, the woman, and the children (clutching their little dog) disappear in seconds. She felt the terror, then the nothingness that remained, all buried and gone.

Mona awoke from the vision. She could not go back to sleep. She picked up the beautiful pendant by her bedside, went to her worktable, and unwrapped the silver wire around it. Then, she laid out a beautiful pattern for a mosaic tabletop. It showed a lovely maiden holding a green vase of flowers, placing it on a table laden with food. Two children and a little dog waited by her side. The green piece of sea glass went into the vase where it truly belonged. It had journeyed across the centuries, across the world, to be at peace.

The tabletop was the most beautiful piece Mona had ever created. But it was not for sale. Mona moved it into her living room and placed a vase full of fresh blooms on it each week for the rest of her life. Their story would not be buried; it would be remembered by one artist who worked in glass.

Imagine

Sometimes I compare

The worries of my past

A mother

Watching from the window

As her son

Ran down the block

To school

How must it have been

For a mother

To watch

A tall ship sail

Out to the endless horizon

To the end o the world

Out to sea?

My block seemed a world away

Full of dangers

Imagine the sea

Where real monsters

Lurked

At

The edge of the world...

I cannot imagine.

The Tiny Mouse and the Sea

Nestled in a rocky crevice lived a very tiny mouse named Simon. He drifted off to sleep by the sound of the waves each evening, and he awoke to the call of the sea birds each morning at daybreak.

"One day, I will sail upon the waves," he softly whispered to himself. He watched the seals climb upon the sand and bask in the sunshine. He watched the tiny crabs crawl amidst the foamy tide. Once, he got a bit too close to the edge and was almost swept away. If only he could move his tiny paws like the seals moved theirs along the sand and the sea. Each day, he scoured the beach grass for berries and seeds. Each night, he dreamed of the sea in the snug little nest he had fashioned out of soft sea grass.

Sometimes, people came to the rocks. Not often, but sometimes brave souls faced the harsh winds and cast long poles out to the sea. The seals didn't visit when people were around. The tiny mouse watched from his nest, too afraid to come out as well. One morning, several men and two little boys came to the beach. The men fished while the boys played at the water's edge with shovels and buckets and toys.

The little mouse was quite hungry by the time they left. Luckily, the people left some food scraps from their lunch littered along the beach. *Quite tasty scraps indeed*, thought the tiny mouse. Then, he spotted it. A shipwreck! Actually, it was a tiny plastic toy boat lying on its side, abandoned by the boys.

What treasure! thought the tiny mouse, squeaking with excitement. He must move it before the tide rose and swept it out to sea. He tugged and tugged with all his might, but it was so heavy. Near exhaustion, the little mouse sat on the rocks and cried.

"Why are you crying?" asked a tiny sandpiper on the beach.

"I am too little to move my sailboat," answered the mouse.

"Your sailboat?" chirped the piper. Then, turning her keen eyes, she saw the plastic boat lying on its side in the sand.

"Hmmmmm," she said. "So, you are a sailor?"

"Oh, yes," squeaked the mouse.

The sandpiper called to her mate, and he soon joined the conversation. The two sandpipers grasped the tiny plastic boat with their beaks and dragged it to a safe crevice in the rocks, turning it upright to squeeze through the opening.

"Oh, thank you, thank you," cried the tiny mouse.

"Safe sailing," chirped the couple as they hurried off to catch some nighttime crawling things on the shoreline.

The tiny mouse climbed aboard his vessel. *She is quite seaworthy*, he proudly sighed. That night, he didn't go back to his nest, instead choosing to sleep aboard his craft.   He watched the moon rise in the sky. He counted each star. He listened to the tide rolling in until, at last, he fell asleep.

Sometimes, tiny mice can journey out to sea, even if they never leave a sheltered place among the rocks. Simon sailed many long journeys of imagination in his tiny mouse life. On his final journey, Simon slowly climbed aboard his ship, very frail and thin. A strong tide rushed upon the shore, pushing the plastic boat away from its mooring in the rocks. Simon wasn't frightened. His eyes had closed in peaceful slumber by then. The plastic boat carried the adventurous sailor out among the waves, out to sea.

Adrift

T he tiny boat wasn't sturdy enough; she capsized in the torrential rain and strong waves. The sea claimed two lives that day. One passenger set adrift, clinging to a piece of her broken hull, all alone in an empty and scary sea. But he wasn't alone.

A mermaid and her little daughter watched the vessel break apart. "We cannot help them," the mother sighed. "They cannot live in the sea, and we cannot be part of the land."

But as the kind pair watched the frightened being clutching to life, they could not swim away. In mermaid song, they called to their friends. Together, they brought pieces of driftwood and strands of seaweed and fashioned a makeshift vessel of their own. The land dweller climbed on board, exhausted, and fell sound asleep. The mother and daughter kept vigil until the storm ceased. "We must bring him some water from the cavern below and some nourishment from the sea." Together, the mother and her child collected food and water and brought it to the hungry survivor.

He drifted for days. In the harshness of the afternoon sun, they lay wet seaweed across his body to shelter him from burns. At night, they protected his tiny vessel from other not-so-friendly beings of the sea that also watched and waited.

Finally, on day four, the mother mermaid spied a large sailing ship on the horizon. "We must leave him now," she cautioned her daughter.

"Oh, mama, can't he stay with us?" she pleaded, having grown quite attached to this strange being of the shore.

"No, we must never let them find us," she said. "Hurry, they will soon take notice of him."

On deck, the captain and his first mate spotted the small object floating on the waves. "Well, I'll be ...." exclaimed the captain, looking through his binoculars. He gave his first mate the strong lens to peer out on the horizon. "Call out to the deck hands. *Man overboard.* Release the life raft." And so they did.

The little mermaid child looked deeply into the eyes of the land dweller. He raised his paw in gratitude, and she held it in her hands. Her little heart would never be the same, now that she had earned the love of a dog.

Mother and daughter watched from a safe distance as the seamen rowed out to the piece of driftwood and carried the little dog on board their raft. They waited until he was safely where he belonged, with the other dwellers of the land.

When night fell, the little mermaid child came up to the surface and found his driftwood vessel. A tuft of fur lay caught in the seaweed strands. She took it, placed it between two shells, threaded her treasure, and wore it close to her heart for the rest of her days.

Sometimes the sea captain and first mate talk about that day amongst themselves.

"Did you see anything strange, sir?" the first mate once asked.

"Dolphins, just dolphins," the captain answered. His first mate never questioned him again.

As for the dog, he found a lovely home by the seaside where he loved to romp among the shoreline and gaze out on to the horizon, perhaps searching for a little girl who loved him.

Love Is Blind

L ong ago, when large ships crossed the ocean currents on billowing sails, a love story like no other began.

A handsome seaman, John Hewitt, stood at his post and saw the approaching clouds. There was little time to prepare. The sails were ripped apart, and the vessel tossed about like a feather in the wind. So many perished that night; the dark sea swallowed them quickly. But the seaman lived. He awoke in darkness, not knowing where he was, or if he was indeed still alive. His eyes were injured; he could not see. His limbs did not feel broken, but his weariness was so great that all he could do was lie still in exhaustion.

Soon, she came. Her voice was lilting, like the sound of the waves. Her touch was soft as she caressed his face and gave him a sip of soup. The soup was salty, different from any he had ever tasted. He was so thirsty, and it was delicious.

"Where am I?"

"You are in a cave. My family brought you here."

"My ship, my mates?"

"They are all gone," she whispered. "Please rest, lie still. I will come back later," she told him. Then, she was gone.

Hours passed. Was it morning? Was it night? He did not know. His mind kept reliving the horrible storm, and sometimes, in brief moments, he thought he saw her in his head. He was struggling in the water. She was so beautiful, with long, raven-colored hair. Then he remembered being struck by a huge plank of wood falling from the hull and all going dark...so dark. He heard her voice calling to him, "I have you. Hold on." Then, all memories were lost, swallowed like his ship on the sea.

She came again, bringing more soup and cool water from a spring within the cave. "What is your name?" he asked. "Where is this place? Am I in England?"

"My name is in a language you would find hard to pronounce, from a place far away from your *England*," she answered. "You whispered that your name is John. Is that so?" she asked.

"Yes, John. John Hewitt," he answered.

"Rest now, John Hewitt," she said, and once more, she was gone.

His memories came again. This time he saw her in his mind. He saw her shimmering tail, the large fins that lapped at the waves. *No, I must be hallucinating*, he thought. *This cannot be. You are in a bed at a hospital in England, you fool!*

When she came again, he reached out his hands to touch her. Startled, she moved back quickly.

"Who are you!" he cried. "What are you?"

"I am a mermaid," she softly answered. He could hear soft sobs as she dropped his bowls of water and soup and slipped away.

Left alone in the darkness, hours passed. "What a fool you are, Hewitt!" he screamed. He tried to stand, but there were so many rocks, he kept cutting himself and falling. "I will die here alone," he whispered to himself and fell off to sleep.

But die alone he didn't. She came back. She came each day for weeks until he was strong again. The two fell in love. The mermaid's family tried to end this relationship, destined for wreck just like the seaman's ship. But she wouldn't listen.

"I want to go with him, back to his England," she told her parents and grandparents.

"You cannot go to his England. You will die."

"Then he will stay here with me," she demanded.

"You cannot keep a man here. He does not belong; he is not one of us!"

The heartbroken mermaid pleaded with her wise grandmother to do something. "Please help us, grandmother. You know all the magick of the sea. I will go to England, even if it means I will die," she wept.

The mermaid's grandmother knew her beloved granddaughter was speaking the truth. She would end her life to go with this man. "Take me to this John Hewitt," she told her granddaughter.

"John, there is someone with me that I want you to meet. This is my grandmother."

Not one to mince words, the grandmother asked the seaman how true his love for her granddaughter was, how much he was willing to give up to remain with her.

"I will give up my human form for her. Can you make me one of you?" he asked.

"No," she answered. "And I cannot give her human form." The mermaid lay sobbing beside her love.

"There is one answer," the old mermaid added. "John, you have no sight, but I can give you sight of a different kind."

Turning toward her granddaughter, she asked, "My beautiful child, are you willing to give up your family for this man?" The beautiful mermaid nodded her head.

"Then you shall travel the sea with songs and clicks that will become your eyes in the darkness. You will sing to us, your family," she told her granddaughter. "We will hear the songs from across the waves and know you are happy and safe."

To this day (though greatly harmed by what was once the family of their ancestral grandfather), their descendants still sing and click their voices in the deep sea. Their voices are their eyes. They sing to the mermaids, telling them that two remained in love until the very end of their days.

The Moon and the Sea

The moon sings to the sea at night...

And if you listen very quietly

In the stillness

You can hear the tides respond

The moon tells the sea of all the stars

She calls for him to make a wish on one

The sea reaches out...

And drifts away again...

The stars forever beyond reach

His waves relentless

In their

Quest to capture one

To wish upon......

And so the song plays on

Each night

The waves outstretched

The stars hiding in the clouds

The moon smiling

The Cruise of a Lifetime

O tter's sign went up by the edge of the marsh. *Cruise to New York City. Deluxe accommodations, seaworthy vessel, affordable rates.*

Captain Milo was a skilled seaman. He was an otter, and otters know the currents. Word soon spread around the marshlands. All the bugs, rats, and mice spread the news.

Seaworthy? Well, that might be stretching the truth a bit. Otter had built his ship securely, that's for sure. It had certainly fared well along the river. But the sea? Well, that was yet to be determined.

The passenger list was growing and growing. Twenty-four mosquitoes, twelve bedbugs, five grasshoppers, six praying mantises, thirty moths, eight crickets, nine fireflies, two walking sticks, six mice, and eleven rats. Soon, Otter's sign read "SOLD OUT."

The voyage was set for the following Tuesday...or, as the swamp told time, the next Full Moon. Tuesday at sunrise, the passengers took board.

"Does everyone have their vaccinations? You never know what you might pick up from blood sucking in New York City," said Captain Milo. He glared at the mosquitoes as he said this.

"Deluxe accommodations," chirped the crickets, "my foot!"

"These beds are hard as rocks!" muttered the bedbugs.

"Listen, do you want to go or not?" answered Captain Milo. "I run a tight ship around here. There are rules. First off, no biting the heads off anyone."

"Ah, gee!!" chirped one praying mantis. "I want my money back!" and off ship she walked.

"We thought this was an all-you-can-eat buffet!" moaned the mosquitoes.

"There will be no blood sucking on my ship," answered Captain Milo. Two mosquitoes flew off in disgust. "Anyone else want to jump ship?" the Captain asked.

And so the voyage began. The fireflies lit their eyes in wide wonder on the moonlit sea. Everyone was up and about. You see, bugs and mice and rats like to stay up all night and sleep during the day. But those darned crickets with all of their racket annoyed everyone.

"Can't we just eat them?" asked the rats.

"NO!!!" said Captain Milo. "I run a safe ship. No one gets eaten on my watch."

"This trip is no fun," squeaked the rodents. "And the food is crummy." Literally crummy, as Captain Milo had provided only crumbs of bread for their sustenance.

"Are we there yet?" buzzed the mosquitoes. "We are starving!" Just like little children, they annoyed the otter to no end.

"Two more moons," he announced on deck the following morning. "Hopefully, the sea will be with us."

But the sea wasn't. Dark storm clouds hung in the western sky, covering up the moon that night. The fireflies lit the darkness as best they could, but all sensed peril was awaiting. The storm came up suddenly. The otter's ship was tossed about in the waves, but she held steady. The rats got seasick, which was pretty disgusting, even for a shipload of bugs.

Finally, they saw her—New York City! Captain Milo skillfully docked his tiny vessel under a bridge piling. "Everyone out!" he yelled.

The two walking sticks stretched their long bodies into gangplanks, and the crawling bugs took off for the sights of the City.

"Be back here with the coming of the next New Moon. Don't be late; we will leave without you!" he admonished.

Quietly, two Asian Beetle stowaways took flight from the lower deck. The moths took off for the garment district. "This is paradise," they fluttered to each other.

The rats and mice found subways and restaurant cellars most appealing. They soon had their first taste of fast food. "This is HEAVEN!!" they squeaked.

The bedbugs took off for the theatre district and all the fancy hotels. "These hotel beds are so soft and scrumptious," they sighed, munching to their hearts' content.

The mosquitoes...well, you know where the mosquitoes went.

The fireflies, grasshoppers, praying mantises, and crickets sped off to Central Park. There, they joined in the concert and cacophony of all the city-dwelling insects.

The New Moon came. "We are missing several mosquitoes, all the bedbugs, and all the rats and mice," Captain Milo stated.

"They aren't coming," came a squeak from the deck.

"We are leaving in ten minutes," announced Captain Milo. And, when the time came, off they went back to the marsh.

"This was a great trip, Captain Milo. Can we do it again next year?" chirped the tired passengers as they crawled and flew off the ship.

"We shall see," said Milo as he heaved a weary sigh. Being Captain was hard work. He was glad to run a tight and safe ship—and glad that all who chose to return home made it safely.

As for those who stayed behind, they started a new life in the Big City, far away from the marshlands of home.

Message in a Bottle

Eve woke up with the sun. Her cottage by the sea was quiet as usual. It was a lovely place, but it had an aura of sadness about it that Eve could never lift, no matter how hard she tried. She planted beautiful roses, she painted cheery colors on the walls, she hung twinkling wind chimes to sing in the breeze; nothing seemed to brighten the heart of her home.

She had bought the cottage five years earlier from the Sawyers. Mr. Sawyer, a man aged beyond his years, told her that his wife used to love the place, used to love the sea. Now, she couldn't bear the sound of the waves at night, couldn't bear to walk on the sand during the day.

"We had a daughter," he said with such sorrow in his eyes. "Jenny," he added. "She was the light of our hearts. One morning, my wife was finishing some kitchen work, loading the dishwasher. Jenny asked to go outside and play in the yard. She was a good girl, always listened to us. My wife told her never to go near the sea, to stay in our garden. Pepper, our little poodle, followed after her. My wife stayed inside for not more than ten minutes. When she went outside and called Jenny, she was gone. Pepper was barking furiously. My wife said the dishwasher had drowned out any sounds from the garden. My wife called me at work, frantic. Jenny had never disobeyed us before; she had never gone near the water without us. She could swim a little, but the tides were strong. We never found her."

His eyes were misted over now. He glanced toward the sea. "I have to get her away from here," he sighed. "I have to get away from here. It's a good, strong cottage. I built it myself. One thing—that angel statue in the garden, we buried Pepper under it. He died a couple of years after we lost Jenny; he never seemed quite the same after, always on guard searching for something. Does that bother you, having him here?"

"Not at all," Eve answered. "Pepper is welcome."

Papers were signed, and the Sawyers rented a small apartment in the village. "Here is our address, in case anything should..." His voice lowered. Eve nodded her head in acknowledgement.

Five years later, the sun shone brilliantly through Eve's bedroom window. Nights were restless lately. She kept hearing a dog barking—the barks of a little dog, high pitched. A couple of nights she had gotten up and gone into the garden to find him. But no dog was there. She smiled, passing by Pepper's grave. "Okay, boy, I hear you. Now, I have to get some more sleep at night."

Eve dressed and strolled on the beach. She worked as an artist, using driftwood, sea glass, and other natural sources for her sculptures and selling them to tourists in the village market. Her eyes were always turned toward the sand, never wanting to miss a treasure. This morning, the gleam of a glass bottle captured her eye. In it, a sheet of paper was rolled into a scroll.

Eve walked back to the house, got a pair of her art tweezers, and lifted it out. "Such beautiful gold writing," she sighed.

Mommy, don't be angry. I listened. I didn't go by the sea. I stayed in the garden like you told me to do. A man came, a mean man. He grabbed my arm and told me to go with him. If I didn't, he told me he would hurt Pepper. He wouldn't stop barking, Mommy. I told him to be quiet like the man said. I was so scared, Mommy. He took me in his car and covered my face so I could not see. He brought me to this place. It is very dark, Mommy. But a kind lady who glows just like my angel nightlight comes to visit me. She has wings, Mommy, just like the sea gulls that fly over our beach. She wraps them around me when I am cold and it makes me warm again. She told me she is taking me home soon. I want to go home, Mommy. I am sorry. The kind lady wrote this for me. She said my heart would say all the right words when she placed the paper in my hands. Did I say all the right words,

Mommy? There's a rooster here, Mommy. I listen to him talk each day. I love you and Daddy.

-Jenny

Eve's heart broke as she read the letter. What should she do? Go to the town constable? With what? A message in an old bottle? She searched about the house for the Sawyers' new address. Were they still living there? She had seen Mrs. Sawyer only once at the village market, and that was years before.

114 Green Briar Lane. That was the address. Eve got her car keys and drove a little faster than the village speed limit allowed. With hesitation, she knocked on the door. No answer. She knocked again. This time, Mr. Sawyer answered. He looked even older than before.

"Can I help you?" he whispered, not recognizing Eve at first. Then, the spark of recognition shone in his eyes, beside a look of bewilderment. "Is there something wrong at the cottage?" he whispered. "We must be quiet," he added. "My wife is sleeping. She has been ill."

Eve took the letter and the bottle from her jacket pocket. "I think you should read this," she told him.

Mr. Sawyer's hands reached for the tiny scroll. "Where did you get this?"

"I found it on the beach this morning," Eve replied.

From the bedroom, a quiet voice asked, "Who is it? What's going on?"

"Nothing, Mary. Just rest."

But Mary wasn't resting. She put on her robe and came into the parlor. At once, she recognized Eve's face. Eve barely recognized her. Her pale face had lost much of its youth and beauty, and dark shadows surrounded her eyes.

"It's about Jenny, I know!" she cried. "I keep dreaming of her." Hesitantly, Mr. Sawyer showed her the letter. "We have to show the town constable. We have to tell him!" she cried.

Mr. Sawyer shook his head. "All this time, Mary, what can he do?"

"I knew my Jenny didn't go into the sea. She was such a good girl." Mrs. Sawyer placed her head in her hands and wept. A sea of emotions swept over her like the tides she had imagined swept over her baby for so many years.

Mary got dressed, and soon the three of them were standing in the constable's office. The constable remembered them, remembered the tragedy.

"We thought you should see this," Mr. Sawyer said.

The constable read the letter. "Hoax, perhaps?" he stated.

"No!" cried Mrs. Sawyer. "It's from Jenny, I KNOW it is!"

The constable read and reread the letter. "Lovely writing, don't you think? Too lovely for any five year old," he added. Then, his eyes fell upon the sentence about the rooster. "May I keep this letter, just for a little while?" he asked the Sawyers. "I want to check something out."

Reluctantly, the Sawyers agreed and left his office. "Miss Sanders, is that your name?" the constable asked.

"Eve," she replied.

"There is something troubling about this letter. I don't want the Sawyers knowing, but I have to pursue an idea I have. I will let you know if anything comes from it."

"Thank you," Eve answered.

The constable rung his superior and asked for a warrant. "Yes, I know grounds for a search warrant are shaky, but I am calling in a favor," he said on the phone.

Two hours later, he was pulling into the Halloran farm, just outside the village. Ted Halloran still lived there; his elderly mom had passed about a year before. The Hallorans used to sell eggs. Neighbors often complained about their pesky rooster crowing in the early morning hours before the sun.

"What's this about?" Ted asked angrily. "Rooster's been dead years now."

"I have a warrant to search your home, Ted."

"Search it for what!?!"

• • •

Pushing the door open, the constable made his way inside the dirty kitchen. He spotted the basement door and started down the dilapidated stairs to the dark, damp cellar. With his flashlight in hand, he shone the beam along the dirt floor. Nothing was down there except some old rags and a bucket. In one corner, the dirt seemed disheveled and out of place with the rest of the soil. Grabbing the bucket, he began lifting pails of soil from the spot. Soon, a tiny skeletal foot poked through the soil.

"Dear God," the constable cried.

Later that afternoon, he drove out to Green Briar Lane first, then to the cottage by the sea.

Eve slept soundly that night, no high-pitched barks to disturb her. The next morning, she went out to the garden, touched the tiny angel statue and whispered, *It's all right now, Pepper. You have been a good boy. We heard you. Now rest with Jenny.* As Eve walked up the back path to her door, the sound of dancing wind chimes echoed in the wind...

With This Ring

Another night, sitting in his chair in the corner of a lonely room. This was his life. The television was blaring; his ears didn't work so well anymore. Some nights it was talk radio. Most nights the television. Some nights just the sound of the waves crashing to shore that soothed the empty space around his house and heart.

They had moved to this sea cottage when he retired. It was their dream. They would garden, gaze at the stars, and take long walks along the coast every day. But the dream didn't last long. She left one drizzly November morning; he awoke and found her very still. Now, his gardening was pushing a broom around the front walkway, tossing the sand out of his path. He didn't look for stars in the night. What was there to wish upon, except the day he joined her once more?

Yes, he had children, all grown now. They had children of their own, starting out careers and dreaming of retirement. Retirement seems like such a glorious dream, until it becomes a lonely nightmare.

Some nights he walks. He rarely sleeps through the night anymore. He never was much for joining community centers or senior citizen clubs. She was the joiner; he was just along for the ride.

His children tried to get him to leave, live in a place with *others* like him. He wondered for whose benefit, his or their own guilt-ridden consciences. But he understood. Life is for the living, those steering the car, not those just along for the ride.

He stored her wedding ring in a little pouch given to him by the funeral director. He kept it on his bedside table. Sometimes, he put it in his pocket to bring her along on his walks by the sea.

She loved the sea.

During the day, the sea was busy with people and children and dogs running at the water's edge. But nights were his and hers alone. He talked to her then. There wasn't much to tell—the latest aches and pains of the previous day, the latest letter from one of their grandchildren, how much he missed her.

The holidays were coming. Holidays were just another day now. He didn't bother with any decorations; presents to his grandchildren were what spare money he could save and place inside an envelope. His children came and stayed at a nearby inn.

"You have to sell this place, Dad," they said. "It is falling apart; it is just too much for you. Sell it while you still can get a good price."

A good price, he thought to himself. That is what mattered after all, wasn't it?

His children left, said they would contact a realtor and to please answer the phone when she called. He nodded. He didn't hear everything they said, but it was easier to nod and wave goodbye.

That night, though cold, he bundled in his hat and scarf, put *her* inside his pocket, and took a walk beneath the stars. His legs ached, but the cold soon numbed the pain a bit. He began his conversation.

"I am a burden, an inconvenience," he sighed.

Just then, a shimmering from the sea edge appeared. A beautiful girl, long flowing hair, in her twenties, shimmered in the moonlight.

"Ask me again," she said, and held out her hand. "My ring, ask me again," she whispered.

"Is it really you?" he cried.

"We have another long journey to begin," she answered.

His fingers reached inside his pocket for the pouch. He took the ring out and reached his hand towards hers...

~~~~~~

The old man's body was found the following morning by neighbors. As for the ring, his daughter searched the house for it in vain. "Foolish, old man," she muttered. "Always losing things. That ring would have paid for your funeral."

The Author at the Beach